Shooting
Star

Bo
(me)

Grandpa

Doug

Alice

Cow

by Bo

Grandpa & Bo

by Kevin Henkes

Greenwillow Books • New York

Pencil was used for the black-and-white art.
The title was hand lettered by Kevin Henkes.
The text type is Cheltenham Book.

Printed in the United States of America
First Edition   10 9 8 7 6 5 4 3 2

Library of Congress Cataloging-in-Publication Data
Henkes, Kevin.   Grandpa and Bo.
Summary: Young Bo spends the summer with his grandfather
in the country and has a wonderful time.
[1. Grandfathers—Fiction.
2. Country life—Fiction]   I. Title.
PZ7.H389Gr 1986   [E]   85-14869
ISBN 0-688-04956-7
ISBN 0-688-04957-5 (lib. bdg.)

For Laura—

the brightest star

Bo was staying with his grandpa for the summer. It was the only time they saw each other all year, except for every other Christmas. Bo lived in the city. Grandpa lived in the country, hundreds of miles away.

They were together all day. They played ball and worked in the garden. They cooked dinner on the grill and ate outside. They listened to Grandpa's old records on the stereo. And they made things—a basket woven of willow switches for Bo's mother. And a statue of a lion carved from soap for Bo's father.

They took long walks through the cornfield behind Grandpa's house. Or short walks if Bo or Grandpa's legs grew tired.

Bo's favorite place was under the big tree that shaded the west end of the house. Sitting there, Grandpa told stories. So did Bo.

Grandpa told about when he was a soldier or about when he was just a boy on Bo's great grandfather's farm. Bo told about when he was just a baby, too little to come to Grandpa's alone.

Beneath the tree, Grandpa taught Bo the names of
things—birds, flowers, grasses.
"What's that?" asked Bo, pointing to a thin green bug.
"That's a praying mantis," answered Grandpa, "but
we can call him Ralph."
Grandpa laughed.
So did Bo.

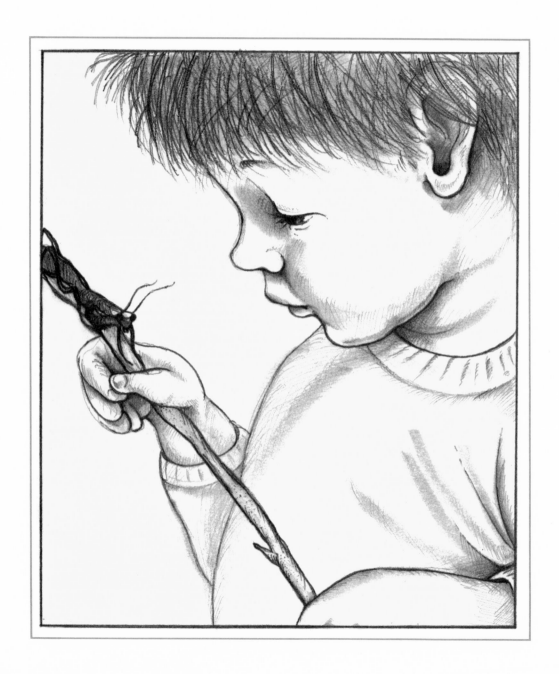

Sometimes they fished under the tree. When Bo caught
three little ones, Grandpa said, "These are blue gills,
but we can call them Tiny, Herb, and Leonard."
But after they named them, Bo didn't want to eat them,
so they threw them back into the lake and had hot
dogs for lunch instead.

We eks passed. Grandpa taught Bo what algae
and garter snakes and gladiolas were. They made faces
at the cows in the neighbor's field. They sat under the
tree watching the branches swish in the wind while the
sun melted into the lake. And they stared at the night
sky, waiting for a shooting star, because Bo had never
seen one.

"What about our tree?" asked Bo one day. "What's his name?"
"He's an evergreen," answered Grandpa. "Mr. Douglas Fir.
But we can call him Doug for short."
Grandpa laughed.
So did Bo.

"I was just thinking, Grandpa," said Bo, looking up at Doug. "I only see you every other Christmas. And you stayed at our house *last* Christmas…"

"Is that so?" said Grandpa. "Then we'll just have to see what we can do about that."

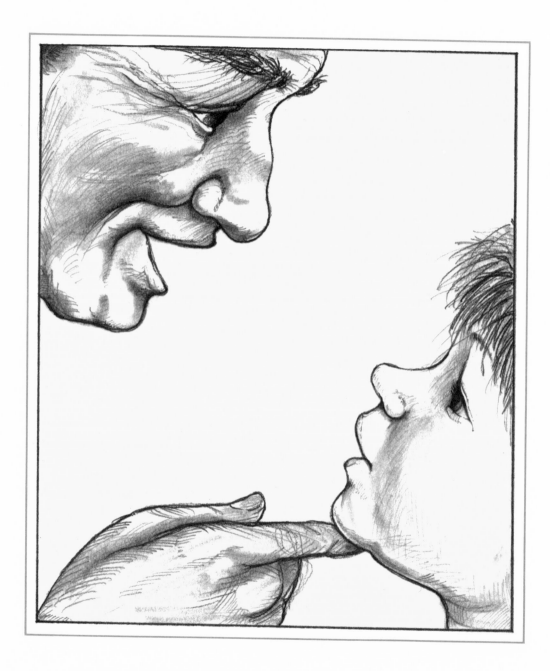

The next morning Grandpa showed Bo how to string
popcorn and berries using a needle and thread. They
hung the popcorn and berries on Doug's low hanging
branches, using a ladder.
"It's for all our birds to eat," said Grandpa. "It's for Goldie
 the finch, Alice the robin, and Herman the sparrow."
"Doug almost looks like a Christmas tree," said Bo.
"I know," said Grandpa.

Grandpa put Christmas carols on the stereo. And they
had turkey and dressing for dinner that night.

"Merry Christmas, Bo," said Grandpa.

"Merry Christmas, Grandpa," said Bo. "Is this *your* first
summer Christmas, too?"

"As far as I can remember," said Grandpa. "And there's
no one I'd rather have it with."

The corn grew. It was up to Bo's ankles when he
came to Grandpa's. Now they had eaten some of the
corn, and the stalks were so tall that Grandpa and Bo
got lost on one of their walks.
The nights were cooler now. The days shorter.
Summer was nearly over and Bo still hadn't seen a
shooting star.

The night before he was to leave, Bo had a hard time sleeping. He got out of bed to look for Grandpa. Bo found him under Doug.

"Bedbugs biting?" asked Grandpa. "Why don't you sit by me?"

So Bo stayed with Grandpa, resting against his shoulder in the chilly night air.

All of a sudden Grandpa shouted, "Look!"

Bo saw a large, bright star streaking across the sky.

"Make a wish," said Grandpa.

"I already did," said Bo. "What did *you* wish?"

"You're not supposed to tell," said Grandpa.

"I bet I know," said Bo.

"I bet you do," said Grandpa. "And you know what else? I bet my wish and yours are exactly the same."

And they were.

Herman

Goldie

Ralph

Herb

Tiny

Leonard